This book belongs to

_____

NEW
Legends
of Aotearoa

New Zealand birds

Irene Swadling

Illustrated by Peter Campbell

REED

Dedicated to the memory of my parents, Cecil and Lillian Lusty,
who shared their love of books, birds and bush with me.

— *Irene Swadling*

For my parents, Angela and John.

— *Peter Campbell*

REED PUBLISHING (NZ) LTD
TE KARUHI TĀ TĀPUI O REED (AOTEAROA)
Established in 1907, Reed is New Zealand's largest
book publisher, with over 600 titles in print.
www.reed.co.nz

Published by Reed Children's Books, a division of Reed Publishing (NZ) Ltd, 39 Rawene Road,
Birkenhead, Auckland 10. Associated companies, branches and representatives throughout the world.

A catalogue record for this book is available from the National Library of New Zealand.

ISBN 13: 978 1 86948 430 9
ISBN 10: 1 86948 430 4
First published 2006

Printed in New Zealand

Contents

How Pīwakawaka found their fans

Way back in the mists of time, there were little birds that lived mainly on the forest floor of Aotearoa New Zealand. Had you met them then, you would have called them 'flat-tails' or 'slow-tails' or 'rere pōturi', because their tails lay behind them.

The flat-tails were friendly, cheerful little birds, but they had one great sadness; their tail feathers dragged them down so they couldn't fly about in the treetops like other small birds.

They were too slow to catch insects on the wing. They had to feed on flies and insects close to the forest floor. They built their nests under fallen forest giants, or in clumps of fern; no treetop nests for them.

'Look how quickly other little birds fly,' sighed Rere Pōturi.

'Our tails make us so slow,' said Tou Pōturi. 'I wish we could really fly.'

'It must be great to catch insects in the air,' added Tou Pāpā.

They could not imagine their wish coming true.

Then one day something happened. They were under a tall tōtara tree, searching through the leaves for food. Suddenly, there was a flurry of feathers. A ruru nestling landed in the leaf litter.

The flat-tails knew this downy, greyish-white chick was too little to leave its nest. The nest was in the clump of epiphytes that clung to the tōtara, high above them.

'I'll go and tell Māmā Ruru at once,' Rere Pōturi cried.

She flew slowly and clumsily to the nest to alert Māmā Ruru. A nestling was snuggled up sleeping in a shallow depression inside the epiphytes. Māmā and Pāpā Ruru were not there!

Māmā and Pāpā had not found enough food for their babies during the night. Just this once they had left their babies alone!

Rere Pōturi returned to her friends.

'Māmā Ruru is not there!' she cried.

A cold breeze stirred the forest floor and Baby Ruru shivered. Rere Pōturi saw that shiver.

'We must look after the baby,' she said. 'Come and make a circle.'

The flat-tails hurried over and made a ring around the little ruru. Facing outward, they gently laid their tail feathers over her. There they stayed, sheltering the baby until the parents returned.

Māmā and Pāpā Ruru did not notice the strange circle of birds beneath their tree. They flew straight into the cluster of epiphytes to feed their chicks.

A melancholy 'more-pork' echoed through the air.

They had found only one nestling!

'Pi, pi, pi, pi!' cried the flat-tails from beneath the tree.

Māmā and Pāpā Ruru quickly flew down.

Slowly and carefully the flat-tails lifted their tails as much as they were able.
They walked forward. There, in the leaf litter, was Baby Ruru, safe and warm.
'Here she is! Here she is!' called Māmā Ruru happily.
'Haere mai, haere mai,' she said as she took her fledgling gently in her
talons. She flew back to the nest.
'Silly little one,' Māmā Ruru said lovingly as she settled her fledgling into the
nest.
'I'll find more food,' called Pāpā Ruru as he flew off.
Their task done, the flat-tails set off in search of insects. They were hungry
after their long sit.
This story might have ended there but it doesn't!
Later that day, Māmā and Pāpā Ruru suddenly remembered they had not
thanked the flat-tails. They felt dreadful. The flat-tails had been so kind.
'We must find some way to reward them,' said Pāpā Ruru. They talked
together for a long time.
Then Māmā Ruru said, 'The flat-tails are always so cheerful, but I do
remember hearing them saying how they wished they could fly quickly like
other small birds.'
Pāpā Ruru replied, 'Āe, I remember that. But we can't grant wishes!'

'No,' said Māmā Ruru quietly, 'but perhaps we could ask Tāne?'

'Ka pai,' cried Pāpā Ruru. 'If we tell Tāne of the flat-tails' great kindness, I'm sure he would help.'

So it was that Māmā and Pāpā Ruru called to Tāne Mahuta, god of the forest. The leaves rustled and a deep, gentle voice was heard.

'What is it you wish? Why do you call on Tāne?'

'Our baby daughter fell from the nest. The flat-tails cared for her and kept her warm. They saved her life. We want to reward them.'

'How can I help with that?' asked Tāne.

'The flat-tails long to fly freely in the forest. Their flat, heavy tails slow them down. Can you help them to fly?'

'I will see that it is done,' replied Tāne, and the ruru were content.

'Thank you, thank you,' they cried.

The next day, as the flat-tails were grabbing grubs from the ground they felt a strange wind behind them. It pushed at their tails. It lifted their tails up little by little, until they were angled up behind them!

Rere Pōturi cried excitedly, 'I feel like I could fly!'

At that moment a gentle voice said, 'Fly now, my little ones, fly.'

Rere Pōturi gave a little run and easily lifted off the ground.

'Come on,' she called to the others.

The gentle voice repeated, 'Fly now, my little ones, fly.'

The others followed Rere Pōturi and lifted off the ground just as easily.

As they went upwards their tails spread out into a fan. It was amazing!

The little birds found they could twist and turn, dart and dive, catch insects on the wing and land easily on a branch or a twig to enjoy their catch.

'Pi, pi!' they cried. 'Who has given us such happiness?'

A gentle voice replied, 'Your kindness has brought you this gift. You cared for the baby ruru. Her parents asked that your dearest wish be granted.'

'Oh, how happy we are,' the little birds cried. 'Our fantails have given us the flying we longed for. Thank you, thank you.'

There was much rejoicing among the little birds as they talked about what had happened. They could not only catch insects on the wing but they could do other things differently as well!

'We can build our nests where we choose,' they sang happily.

And choose they did. Male and female worked together to make their neat cup-shaped nests anywhere from one metre to 24 metres above the ground. It is not surprising that some stayed close to the forest floor. They were just not used to living up high. Nor is it surprising that they continued to use the dry wood from rotting logs, grasses, moss and cobwebs to make their nests.

To this day these little birds, now called pīwakawaka, or fantails, can open and close their tails as they wish.

Tūī and the trees: food for a song

Once, in the deep forest long ago, all the trees of Tāne blossomed at the same time.

Each spring the trees would break out into spectacular reds, sunny yellows and sparkling whites. It was a time of great beauty and harmony.

As time went by, however, the trees changed. Where once they had greeted each other with joy at their flowering, vanity spoiled the harmony. The trees became vain and boastful.

'Look at my wonderful red flowers,' cried Pōhutukawa.

'Red flowers are nothing compared to my yellow,' retorted Kōwhai.

Other trees joined the argument. Only Pūriri tried to remind them of each other's beauty.

When Tūī sang, however, the boasting stopped. All the trees listened with delight.

The trees agreed that Tūī brought a special joy. They loved the melodious songs that filled the air around them.

'Come and sing from my branches,' they would invite when Tūī paused to rest.

Sometimes Tūī arrived to hear Kōwhai and Pōhutukawa arguing. When this happened Tūī scolded them roundly, gurgling and clucking in her throat. The arguing stopped at once.

As summer approached, the trees began to lose their flowers. Petals lay scattered on the ground and the Tūī became cross. They gurgled and clucked to each other, complaining about the trees.

Late one summer, after a sad and sulky talk with his friends, Tūī called to the trees, 'Why do you all blossom at the same time? Where can we drink the sweet nectar of your flowers now?'

The trees were shocked.

'Springtime is the time for flowering. That is why we flower together. How could we admire each other if we flowered at different times?'

'Admire each other!' scoffed Tūī. 'You don't admire each other. Each of you claims to be the most beautiful. It is self, self, self.'

The trees stood stunned and silent. Tūī was right.

'We have been boastful,' they murmured sadly.

Tūī clucked and scolded. 'If you really loved us you would agree to flower at different times.'

Then the tūī flew away from the forest to search for late-blooming harakeke. Flax flowers and insects would have to do.

The trees were stunned. 'Do the tūī really believe we don't love them? How can we change?'

In autumn the tūī returned. They returned to the tall tōtara and stately kahikatea trees. They feasted on their berries and sang joyously.

When the berries were gone, Tūī turned to the trees of the forest and said, 'Oh tamariki of Tāne, who will flower for us this winter? Mātāriki is coming. Who will bring forth flowers for the New Year?'

The trees whispered and rustled together.

'Not us,' called the kōwhai. 'We are definitely a spring tree. We lose our leaves as well as our flowers, so we have much work to do. We must have our winter sleep to form flower buds and leaf buds. We must flower in spring.'

'We too must wait for spring,' Rewarewa sighed. 'Our red and yellow flowers are so curled and complicated.'

'Perhaps Rata could wait until summer,' Pōhutukawa proposed.

'We could possibly do that if you wait too,' Rata responded.

And so all the pōhutukawa and the rata agreed to blossom in summer.

Tūī sang a few joyous notes. Now they were assured of nectar in spring and summer. The rich berries of kahikatea and tōtara satisfied them in autumn. Only the problem of winter remained.

Tūī turned to look at old Pūriri. Pūriri felt flushed and uncomfortable. Mātāriki was coming. In the time of Mātāriki the move towards longer days began. After the dreamtime of the longest night, would Mātāriki want their blossoms in her growing time?

The pūriri looked at each other. They rustled and nodded.

Feeling rather pink and embarrassed, they said to Tūī, 'We love your singing. We are happy that you drink our nectar and spread our pollen. We will try to blossom this winter.'

All the tūī sang for joy and the pūriri immediately settled to their task.

Pūriri panted and pushed. Pink with the pushing they produced early buds.

Pink buds! The buds opened into pink flowers.

Tūī now had food from the trees all year through. From that time, deep in the long ago, the trees have provided food fit for the songs that the tūī sing.

The tūī still sometimes chuckle and chortle and scold for that is the way of the tūī. Tūī also enjoy eating insects and visiting the orange flowers of harakeke. But, the tūī always remember the place in the forest where flowers are found.

As for the trees, instead of arguing, they now have time to admire each other's beauty.

From time to time, however, they cannot resist teasing Pūriri about those once-white flowers turned pink with effort and embarrassment at the time of changing.

Pūriri does not mind at all. Not only because it is from her winter blossoms that the tūī sings so joyously; Pūriri is also able to grow some blossoms all year round.

Kōwhai and Rewarewa know their time is coming in spring. Pōhutukawa and Rata wait patiently for summer, when Tūī will join them. Then, during the shortening days of autumn, these friends listen together for the melodious songs of the tūī as they feed from the berries of Tōtara and Kahikatea.

And so it is that the trees live in harmony, and all tūī are able to give song for food year round.

A hood for Ngiru-ngiru

Long, long ago, somewhere back in the mists of time, Tawhairauriki gave a very special gift to a tiny bird of South Island, Aotearoa New Zealand.

This is the story of Mīharo, a ngiru-ngiru, or tit, and his special friend, the mountain beech tree, Tawhairauriki.

Mīharo was a cheeky, cheerful, trilling little bird. His parents and brothers and sisters made a big fuss of him. He had been the last chick to hatch from his parents' second batch of eggs, late one February morning.

'Look, Father,' Mother Ngiru-ngiru trilled that morning. 'Our last chick has hatched.'

Father looked. 'Amazing,' he said as he studied the tiny chick. 'We will call him Mīharo.'

Mīharo was indeed a very small chick, but he had an enormous appetite. He kept his parents busy bringing grubs and insects. He grew quickly. When the time came for flying, he was fit and strong.

Mīharo was adventurous. He loved exploring the beech forest.

'I'm so happy. I'm so lucky,' he trilled as he flittered and fluttered further and further from the nest.

His zest for living and sense of adventure made Mīharo a favourite of the beech trees he visited. He chattered and chittered as he chased insects through the forest.

'Mīharo, how fast you fly,' the trees would say as he paused in his flying.

'Yes,' Mīharo replied. 'I catch lots of insects as I fly. Look how I am growing.'

Tawhairauriki, an old, old tree with a trunk covered in the thick, black velvety fungus that dripped honey, kept a special eye on Mīharo. Tawhairauriki grew high on the mountainside and sometimes worried that Mīharo was too adventurous.

'Little Mīharo,' he said, 'you are a long way from your nest. Beware of sudden storms.'

'What is a storm?' trilled Mīharo cheerfully.

'It is when the cold wind of the south blows with all his strength.'

'I will beware,' replied Mīharo. Then he flitted off to visit other trees. He investigated everything from the moss and ferns on the forest floor to the leathery leaves of the high mountain beech trees.

One day Mīharo, having eaten his fill of grubs and insects, was attracted by the sun. It shone in slanting, sparkling lines down through the forest. Mīharo followed the slanting lines of sunshine up through the trees to where Tawhairauriki stood, near the top edge of the forest. Tawhairauriki, with his shorter trunk and thick leathery leaves, had often seen storms.

'The sky is blue today, little Mīharo, but beware the sudden storms. The cold wind brings snow and the icy glaciers grow,' said Tawhairauriki.

'I will beware,' called Mīharo.

The days were getting shorter and Mīharo was kept busy gathering food. He learned how to set a nest in the hollow of a tree trunk.

'What do I need?' he asked his parents.

'Find moss and bark. Bring cobwebs. Make a warm shelter. Line it with feathers,' they replied.

Then, one blue morning, the nest was done. Mīharo celebrated by flying off to visit his friends. He flew further and further up through the forest, enjoying moments of cheery chatter with both birds and bush. He quite forgot Tawhairauriki's warning.

'Oh, look,' Mīharo gasped cheerily. 'This must surely be snow.' He flew out of the bush and looked with amazement at the soft white petals that reached into the forest.

For the first time he left the shelter of the trees and flew higher than before, across a ridge to where a glacier of ice interrupted the smooth carpet of snow. The glacier was cut about and deep blue gleamed in the crevasses below him.

'How beautiful,' Mīharo exclaimed as he flew down the river of ice.

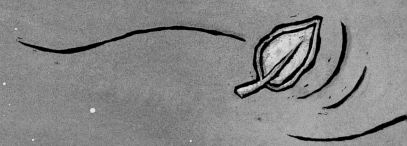

Suddenly, a dark shadow dimmed the snow.

Looking up he cried, 'Te Rā, Te Rā, where are you?', for the sun had vanished. Leaden clouds covered the sky and little white flakes began to fall.

'I must hurry back to the forest,' cried Mīharo. At that instant the cold south wind began to blow. It buffeted Mīharo as a blanket of falling snow blotted out his vision.

A feeling of fear filled him. 'I must keep my head,' thought Mīharo bravely. 'I must fly upwards.'

Mīharo's wings felt stiff and heavy as the wind and snow pushed him this way and that. Slowly and steadily he made progress. With great determination he managed to cross over the ridge. Through a gap in the storm he caught a glimpse of his beloved beech forest.

In the whirling and blurring of the snowflakes Mīharo searched for his friends, the beech trees.

Suddenly, a great creaking and roaring reached his ears.

'Tawhairauriki, Tawhairauriki is calling me,' exclaimed Mīharo.

Mīharo struggled through the wind and snow. He was tiring and flying was becoming more difficult. A gust of wind picked him up and flung him around. He felt trapped and helpless.

'Tawhairauriki,' he sobbed, 'I need your help. I need your help.'

The wind tried to rush him past his friend, but Tawhairauriki reached out with twiggy, leathery fingers and snatched Mīharo from the wind.

'Oh thank you, thank you,' cried trembling Mīharo. 'You told me to beware but I forgot!' He sank into a hollow in the trunk.

Mīharo was shivering with cold and Tawhairauriki was concerned.

'Cuddle close, Mīharo,' he said, 'I will soon have you warm.'

With twiggy fingers the old beech tree worked quickly to weave a wonderfully warm hood from the black velvet coating his trunk. He fitted it over Mīharo's head, shoulders and upper back.

Mīharo began to feel warm again and his shivering stopped.

'Oh Tawhairauriki,' he said. 'I was so frightened. I was so cold. Now I am warm and safe. My hood feels wonderful. I will never take it off.'

Down in the lower beech forest, Mīharo's family waited anxiously.

'Where is Mīharo?' they asked each other. 'There is a storm. Oh, we do hope he has not got caught in the storm.'

Late in the day when the storm had passed, little Mīharo fluttered back to join his family.

'Where did you get your lovely hood?' his brothers exclaimed. Mīharo told them about his adventure and how his friend Tawhairauriki had saved and warmed him.

'How we wish we could have a hood like yours,' sighed his brothers.

'I will ask Tawhairauriki,' said Mīharo. 'Perhaps his friends could make them for you.'

Mīharo was right to trust Tawhairauriki. It was not long before all the male ngiru-ngiru were fitted with beautiful black hoods.

And so it is that male ngiru-ngiru wear their black hoods to this very day.

The three parrots

Once upon a time, a very long time ago, three parrots lived in the forest of Aotearoa New Zealand. Their names were Tahi, Rua and Toru.

Tahi and Toru were brothers, and Rua was their sister. Tahi and Toru were very vain and boastful.

'Look at my lovely green feathers,' boomed Tahi. 'No one else has feathers as green as mine.'

'Just look at the red under my wings,' screeched Toru. 'It's brighter than the sunset.'

They squabbled all day long. Tūī and Korimako couldn't hear themselves sing, and Kererū choked on her berries.

'Please, Rua,' they begged, 'make your brothers stop that noise.'

Rua tried. 'Everyone is different,' she said quietly to her brothers. 'Please don't squabble.' But Tahi and Toru took no notice of her.

'My feathers are much softer than yours,' boasted Tahi.

'But look at those ugly brown marks,' scoffed Toru. 'My red feathers are much more beautiful!'

'Don't be stupid!' said Tahi. 'They're hidden under your wings. No one can see them there!'

They screeched and squawked for hours. The other birds grew angry.

'You must do something, Rua,' said Tūī. 'Your brothers are ruining our forest. We don't want to listen to them squabbling all the time.'

'I'll try,' she said sadly, 'but they won't listen to me.'

Rua flew down to a clearing where Tahi and Toru were strutting and prancing and screaming at each other.

'Please stop this,' she cried. 'Don't you know that we birds are all beautiful?'

Tahi and Toru turned and laughed at Rua. 'You,' scoffed Toru, 'you think you're beautiful?'

'Look at those dull brown feathers,' laughed Tahi. 'Who'd want to look at you?'

Rua hunched up miserably as they went on screeching. Then she had an idea. She would go and ask Tāne Mahuta, god of the forest, to help her.

Rua flew to the top of a tall tōtara. 'Please, Tāne,' she called, 'please will you listen to me?'

A wind rustled the branches. From the rustling came the deep, gentle voice of Tāne. 'What is it, Rua?'

'My brothers are always boasting about how beautiful they are,' said Rua. 'They quarrel and screech and squawk all day long. I've tried to stop them boasting, but they won't listen to me. What can I do?'

'You've done your best, Rua,' said Tāne. 'Leave it to me now.' And he disappeared into the undergrowth.

Tahi and Toru were there, screeching at each other as usual.

'Tahi!' thundered Tāne, his voice stern. 'You have been vain and boastful. From now on you will be called Kākāpō, the night parrot. You will only come out when it is dark. No one will see your beautiful green feathers. You will make your nest in burrows and cracks in the rock. No more flying around in the treetops for you!'

Toru tried to scramble off into the ferns, but there was no escaping Tāne.

'As for you, Toru, I rename you Kea. You can take your shrieking up into the mountains, far away from the forest. You can search around up there for berries and insects, but the riches of the forest are not for you.'

Then Tāne turned to Rua.

'Rua, you have done your best to make our forest a place of beautiful birdsong once more. I name you Kākā, parrot of the bush.'

Kākāpō is still proud of the soft green of his feathers, and Kea is still boastful. 'I am the only mountain parrot in all the world!' he screeches. Nobody minds because the noise soon dies away across the mountainsides.

Kākā is free to enjoy the peace of the forest. Sometimes she misses her brothers, but if she flies to the tops of the tallest trees she can hear Kea's voice screeching down from the mountains. And, late at night, she can sometimes hear the sound of Kākāpō's deep voice booming out in the darkness of the forest.

And so it was that Kākā, Kea and Kākāpō were separated, never again to live together in the forest.

Kākāpō, parrot of the night

Once upon a time, a very long time ago, a parrot was banished from the daytime forest of Aotearoa New Zealand. He and his brother had caused a constant commotion.

'Tahi, I rename you Kākāpō,' Tāne had thundered. 'You will now be a parrot of the night and live on the ground.'

'Banished,' muttered Kākāpō, 'banished to the night and the forest floor.'

Stunned and saddened, Kākāpō searched for a place to sleep. Kākāpō had no choice but to sleep during the day from then on.

When Kākāpō awoke from his first day-sleep, Marama the moon sent soft beams of reflected light to the forest floor. Kākāpō stared up through the trees to the night sky. Stars twinkled and blinked in a blanket of black.

Kākāpō looked down at his soft, green feathers, still visible in the moonlight.

'Oh, my feathers,' he said, 'I should not have boasted so of your beauty. This night-time is special, but where will I find a friend?'

Kākāpō was feeling very alone.

He heard a small sound. It sounded like 'kee-wee'. He saw a shadowy shape on thick, strong legs in the night light ahead.

'Pō mārie,' he called.

The brown shape lifted a long beak and cried, 'Haere atu! Go away! This is my patch!' It was Kiwi.

The brown shape ran at Kākāpō on strong, large clawed feet.

Kākāpō ran back the way he had come.

Feeling more alone than ever, Kākāpō looked around.

'I'm so hungry,' he thought, 'I'd better find something to eat.'

Kākāpō found plenty of berries and ferns, rhizomes and seeds on the lower layers of the forest floor. There were rich pickings to be had off fallen forest giants, which acted as hosts to many small plants.

The next night Kākāpō was once again looking for a friend. A kiore ran past his feet. Kākāpō called to him hopefully, but Kiore replied, 'No, must hide, must hide. Ruru will be hunting.'

He scampered away and Kākāpō was left alone again.

With no brother to quarrel with, Kākāpō spent his nights eating and his days sleeping. He grew lazier and lazier. He never felt the need to fly.

One night Kākāpō found some very interesting little plants on the trunk of a tree.

'Yum,' he thought, sidling up the trunk, eating as he went.

'Oh, my,' he thought after a while, 'tino pai te kai! I'm really full.' He fluttered to the ground.

'That's funny, my wings feel shorter. Must need my sleep. It's nearly dawn. I'm back to my burrow.'

Kākāpō had found a burrow in the roots of a tree. He no longer nested in the treetops of the forest.

Not long after this, Kākāpō climbed high into a tree, eating as he went.

'No friend, no friend,' he sighed between each mouthful.

Then he heard the call of the ruru. 'Roo-roo, more-pork, roo-roo.'

'Maybe Ruru will be my friend,' he thought. He followed Ruru's call, but Ruru was not happy when Kākāpō appeared.

He swooped over Kākāpō, talons outstretched.

'I am an owl, you are a parrot,' he hooted. 'I have no time for you. I am hunting my dinner.'

Then he swooped down through the bush towards the forest floor.

Kākāpō remained where he was, picking at the delicious food around him. Towards morning he fluttered to the ground.

'My wings don't work so well; I seem to be getting heavy,' he boomed.

Once again, Kākāpō clawed his way towards some delicious young leaves. As dawn approached, he found himself high in a tree.

He fluttered down awkwardly, landing safely but heavily.

'I think I'll do some flying,' he thought to himself.

He stretched out his wings and flapped. But he did not fly.

He stretched out his wings carefully and flapped energetically. But still he did not fly.

For a third time Kākāpō tried to fly. He stretched his wings, flapped them and ran forward. But still he did not fly.

Then the words of Tāne came back to him.

'You will make your nest in burrows and cracks in the rocks. No more flying in the treetops for you!'

Kākāpō bowed his head in sorrow and stumbled back to his burrow.

That day he slept uneasily. In the evening he failed to notice the beauty of the night.

'Oh, Tāne, how I am punished!' sobbed Kākāpō.

He climbed and clawed and clambered his way up on to a tree branch.

Filling his lungs with air, he boomed his sorrow out into the night.

He boomed and boomed.

Tāne heard Kākāpō's sorrow and felt great aroha towards him.
Through the dark forest he sent Pai to Kākāpō. Pai was a beautiful female
and she was to be a mate for Kākāpō.
'Kākāpō, I heard you call,' said Kākāpō Pai. 'I have come to be your mate.
What soft, green feathers the moonlight shows me.'
'Ko wai koe? What is your name?' asked Kākāpō. 'Who has sent you?'
'Ko Kākāpō Pai au. Tāne has sent me to you,' said Kākāpō Pai.
'Oh, Kākāpō Pai, I am so happy,' sighed Kākāpō. 'You are beautiful like me
and a great gift from Tāne.'

Kākāpō is still a night parrot. He still lives on the forest floor. Flying is not for
him.
But now he is happy again. Happy and proud of his soft, green feathers,
happy that his booming can bring a mate, and proud that he is now the
heaviest parrot in all the world.

Note: Although kākāpō have remained ground parrots, the forest floor
became a dangerous place for them when cats and dogs came to
Aotearoa New Zealand. Today, kākāpō are a protected species and live in
bird sanctuaries on offshore islands.

Kea is found

Once, in the days of long ago, no parrots lived in the mountains of Aotearoa New Zealand. They were all bush or forest dwellers.

Toru, the ancestor of the mountain parrots, was moved to the mountains by Tāne. Had he remained alone this story would not have been written. But, back in the bush, a little band of similar parrots really missed Toru.

'Where is Toru?' his friends complained. 'It's no fun without him.'

'Tāne has banished him to the mountains,' said Pōtiki, the youngest parrot. 'I heard Tāne rename him Kea. Tāne said no one would mind Kea's noise in the mountains.'

'We must go and find him. He will be lonely without us.' Although Toru had been noisy and quarrelsome with his brother Tahi, his friends found him fun to be with.

'Where are the mountains?' asked Whero.

'I don't know,' sighed Pōtiki. Then he brightened. 'My friend Aroha the moa will know.'

So it was that the little group went in search of Aroha. They flew in and out of the trees crying, 'Haere mai, Aroha, haere mai.'

Pōtiki spotted Aroha in her favourite clearing near a stream. She was shearing away at a bush with her sharp beak. She looked enormous. Pōtiki suddenly felt very small, even though she knew Aroha was her friend.

Aroha saw Pōtiki hesitate and she stopped eating. 'What is it, Pōtiki?' she asked gently.

'Tāne has sent Toru to the mountains. We want to go there too.'

'It's a long way,' said Aroha.

'But do you know the way?' asked Whero.

'You must travel south until you come to the large river,' Aroha replied. 'The river comes from the west. Follow that river.'

'Will that take us to the mountains?' the little parrots asked.

'Follow the river to the lake, go around the lake until you find the river again. Eat well and rest on the way,' Aroha advised. 'There will be dangers. If you see other moa, show them this feather.'

Aroha handed Pōtiki one of her fluffy, reddish-brown feathers.

'Thank you, Aroha,' said Pōtiki.

'Respect Tāwhirimatea. He may send sudden storms. Watch for Harpagornis the eagle.'

'We will.'

'Your flight to the mountains will be long and hard. I wish you luck. Hāere rā, friends of Toru.'

'E noho rā, Aroha. Kia ora koe. Thank you for your help.'

Chattering and excited, the parrots set off to the south. They flew below the high forest canopy, crossing small clearings and streams. Late in the day they flew down to a clearing where some moa were feeding. The large birds looked curiously at the little group.

'I haere koutou? Where are you going?'

'To the mountains. We need to find the large river. Will we reach it today?' they asked.

'The river is a long way. We see you carry a feather of friendship. Stay near us tonight. We will make sure Harpagornis does not trouble you.'

At the mention of Harpagornis all the moa looked round anxiously. They searched the sky for eagles' wings before continuing to feed.

'Does Harpagornis trouble you?' asked Pōtiki.

'Yes, he is our enemy. If we are not careful one of us could be carried away in his strong talons.'

At that moment there was a loud cry. 'Danger!'

The birds raced for the trees. The moa family bent their necks low to the ground and pushed their way into the undergrowth.

Pōtiki crouched, trembling, under the trees. Gazing out, he saw the shadow of giant wings and a cruel and ugly beak. It must be Harpagornis!

The next morning the travelling parrots were ready early.

'E noho rā, koutou,' they cried to the moa family as they circled around above them. 'Thank you for a good night.'

'Haere rā, e manu iti. Fly well.'

The little group flew across the stream and continued southwards. Once again they flew under the forest canopy, away from the searching eyes of Harpagornis.

Many curious bush birds called to them, 'Where are you going?'

The reply was always the same. 'Ki ngā maunga — to the mountains.'

Towards the end of the day they flew out of the trees and stopped, stunned.

'He awa — the river, he maunga — the mountains. Look at the colours!'

Flying to the tops of the trees, they gazed in amazement. The river, reflecting the colours of the sunset, threaded its way through a wide gravel bed. To the west white peaks and rugged ranges were outlined against a blue and orange sky.

'We must rest here tonight,' cried Pōtiki. 'Eat well. Tomorrow we follow the river!'

During the night a strong wind began to blow. The parrots stirred restlessly as branches swayed and swung. By dawn a hard relentless rain was being driven into the trees by the gale-force wind.

The parrots were dismayed. 'Oh no. Tino kino te hau! We did not thank Tāwhirimatea.'

'We cannot travel today,' said Pōtiki.

The parrots turned sadly to struggle through the swaying trees. They sought out a spot where the storm's ravages no longer reached them.

As they huddled together deep in the bush, they listened to the rage of Tāwhirimatea. Uprooted trees crashed and fell where river plain and forest met.

'We are sorry, Tāwhirimatea!' cried the parrots. 'We forgot to thank you.'

By nightfall the forest was still.

After a damp and uncomfortable night the parrots woke to a fresh dawn.
'Thank you, Tāwhirimatea,' they cried as they returned to the river.
'Is this the river?' they asked in dismay as they looked at the muddy, swirling water.
'We cannot see the mountains!' others cried. The mountains were hidden in cloud.
'We follow the river,' Pōtiki reminded them. 'We must be brave.'
So the parrots continued their journey to search for Toru. They followed the river, reached the lake and flew round the shoreline. Wading birds greeted them. Another day took them up a smaller river to the bottom of a waterfall.
'We must rest here,' said Whero.
'Tomorrow we will find Toru,' they said.
The next morning, from the shade of the deep valley, they looked up at a blue sky. The river dropped down from above them in a great fall.
'Today we will be in the mountains,' they sang as they flew up the face of the fall.
The parrots cleared the top of the falls, then stopped in wonder. The white peaks were now so much closer.

As they paused, a sound they knew reached them.

'Kee-aaa, kee-aaa, kee-aaa,' came the cry.

'Toru!' they exclaimed. 'Kee-aaa, kee-aaa,' the group replied.

Joyously they soared upward towards the black speck that had to be Toru!

Then Toru was in their midst. 'Haere mai. Folllow me. You are so clever to find me,' Toru said.

They followed Toru to the place where yellow tussock and white snow met.

Here there were insects to eat and snow to play in.

The little parrots told Toru how much they had missed him and how they had decided to search for him.

'You must take my name, Kea,' cried Toru. 'It's so good to see you. Tāne sent me here. Now you have found me. What good times we will have together.' And so it was that the mountain parrots became many. They revelled in the space and freedom of the mountains. There were hard times when storms raged, but flying freely and frolicking in the snow made up for that.

Today the name of Toru is almost forgotten. All his descendants are known as 'kea' because of the call they make. Frolicking, feeding and fooling, they remain in the mountains — the only mountain parrots in all the world.

Glosssary of words and phrases

How Pīwakaka found their fans

Tou Pōturi	Slow Tail
Tou Pāpā	Flat Tail
ruru	morepork, New Zealand owl
epiphytes	plants that grow on other plants
Haere mai	Welcome
āe	yes
ka pai	very good
Tāne Mahuta	god of the forest
tōtara	New Zealand red pine

Tūī and the trees: food for a song

pōhutukawa	sometimes called the New Zealand Christmas tree
kowhai	yellow; a native tree of New Zealand
pūriri	a native tree of New Zealand, related to teak
harakeke	New Zealand native flax
kahikatea	New Zealand white pine
tamariki of Tāne	children of Tāne
Mātāriki	the Māori New Year
rewarewa	honeysuckle
rata	New Zealand mistletoe

A hood for Ngiru-ngiru

tawhairauriki	mountain beech tree
mīharo	amazing
te rā	the sun

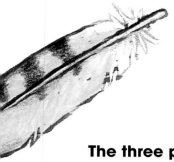

The three parrots

tahi	one
rua	two
toru	three
korimako	bellbird
kerurū	New Zealand native pigeon
kākāpō	the night parrot
kea	mountain parrot
kākā	parrot of the bush

Kākāpō, parrot of the night

Marama	the moon
pō mārie	good evening
haere atu	go away
rhizomes	horizontal plants with shoots above and roots below
kiore	Pacific rat
tino pai te kai	the food is great
Ko Kākāpō pai au.	I am Kākāpō Pai.

Kea is found

pōtiki	youngest
aroha	love
Tāwhirimatea	god of wind and storms
Harpagornis	a now extinct eagle that used to live in New Zealand
haere rā	goodbye (to those leaving)
e noho rā	goodbye (to those staying)
kia ora koe	thank you
e noho rā, koutou	goodbye to you all
haere rā, e manu iti	goodbye, little birds
tino kino te hau	the wind is really bad

About the author

Irene Swadling is a mother, grandmother and teacher. Born and raised in Wellington, she developed an early love of New Zealand flora and fauna when she was exploring Wilton's Bush (now Otari Nature Reserve) near her home.

Irene and her husband Harry have tramped many of New Zealand's national and forest parks. She is a member of the New Zealand Forest and Bird Society and The Karori Wildlife Sanctuary.

Irene has dabbled in writing for as long as she can remember. She has written and produced children's plays and operettas at schools and churches among other things, and continually entertains her three children and seven grandchildren with a variety of poems and stories.

About the illustrator

Peter Campbell lives in Wellington and has been working as an illustrator for over 10 years. He has illustrated many works, including titles in the 'Wild Stories' series by Andrew Crowe for Heinemann Education. He has also illustrated books for other educational publishers in New Zealand, England and Australia.

Peter is largely self-taught and uses print-based techniques in much of his work. He has exhibited prints works in New Zealand and overseas.

In this book, Peter used the ink resist technique to create the line work. This technique is similar to that used to make linocuts. The images have been coloured with a variety of media, including inks and coloured pencils.